Hairy Maclary and Zachary Quack

Lynley Dodd

PUFFIN

It was drowsily warm,
with dozens of bees
lazily buzzing
through flowers and trees.
Hairy Maclary decided to choose
a space in the shade
for his afternoon
snooze.
He dozily dreamed
as he lay on his back
when …

pittery pattery,
skittery scattery,
Z I P
round the corner
came
Zachary Quack

who wanted to frolic
and footle
and play
but …

Hairy Maclary
skedaddled
away.

Over the lawn
and asparagus bed
went Hairy Maclary
to hide in the shed.
He lurked in the shadows
all dusty and black
but …

pittery pattery,
skittery scattery,
Z I P
round the corner
came
Zachary Quack.

Out of the garden
and into the trees
jumped Hairy Maclary
with springs
in his knees.
He hid in the grass
at the side of the track
but …

pittery pattery,
skittery scattery,
Z I P
round the corner
came
Zachary Quack.

Down to the river
through willow and reed
raced Hairy Maclary
at double the speed.
Into the water
he flew with a
S M A C K
but …

pittery pattery,
skittery scattery,
Z I P
round the corner
came
Zachary Quack,
who dizzily dived
in the craziest way,
whirling
and swirling
in showers of spray.

Hairy Maclary
was off in a flash,
a flurry of bubbles,
a dog paddle splash.
He swam to the side
and floundered about,
he tried
and he tried
but he C O U L D N ' T
climb out.
Scrabbling upwards
and slithering back …
when

pittery pattery,
skittery scattery,
Z I P
through the water
came
Zachary Quack,
who sped round a corner
and,
showing the way,
led Hairy Maclary
up, up
and away.

Then,
soggy and shivering,
back up the track
went Hairy Maclary
with
Zachary Quack.

It was drowsily warm,
with dozens of bees
lazily buzzing
through flowers
and trees.
Hairy Maclary
decided to choose
a place in the shade
for his afternoon
snooze.
He dozily dreamed
as he lay on his back …

tucked up together
with
Zachary Quack.

PUFFIN BOOKS

UK | USA | Canada | Ireland | Australia | India | New Zealand | South Africa
Puffin Books is part of the Penguin Random House group of companies
whose addresses can be found at global.penguinrandomhouse.com.

www.penguin.co.uk   www.puffin.co.uk   www.ladybird.co.uk

Penguin
Random House
UK

First published in New Zealand by Mallinson Rendel Publishers Limited 1999
Published in Great Britain in Puffin Books 2001
Reissued 2010
001

Text and illustrations copyright © Lynley Dodd, 1999
All rights reserved
The moral right of the author/illustrator has been asserted

Made and printed in China

ISBN: 978–0–141–33516–2